The Beatinest* Boy

Beatinest—surpassing all others, most unusual.

WEBSTER

The

WHITTLESEY HOUSE
McGraw-Hill Book Company, Inc.
NEW YORK   TORONTO   LONDON

Beatinest Boy

JESSE STUART

Illustrated by
ROBERT HENNEBERGER

Copy 1

Library of Congress Catalog Card Number: 53-11490

Published by Whittlesey House

a division of the McGraw-Hill Book Company, Inc.

Printed in the United States of America

III

To
GENE DARBY
my nephew

CONTENTS

The Cry on the Mountain

David took long steps as he walked down the winding path through the cow pasture. He had told his Grandma Beverley that he was going to climb this mountain, go up to the top and stick his hand through a cloud. Grandma said she was too tired and that she wanted to go to bed early. Maybe she just wanted to let me go alone, David thought.

David was sure his Grandma Beverley was the smartest, most wonderful woman in the world. She could do just about anything. Ever since his father and mother had died and he'd come to live with her, she had been teaching him wonderful things. He hadn't liked the idea of going to live with the tall strange woman, but

9

he and she were a real family now. She had shown him how to hunt, how to keep chickens and the cow, how to plant potatoes and corn, and how to use a long-handled gooseneck hoe.

Grandma must have felt that he was a great help to her—in fact, didn't she often say he was the beatinest boy in the world and she couldn't get along without him? Grandma never fussed and she knew an awful lot of useful things.

David climbed higher and higher. He looked through the thin mist above him and he could see the setting sun. Then he put his hand up through the mist and felt the warm rays of the sun. "My hand is through the cloud," he shouted.

Then he took a few more steps and he was standing above the sea of clouds that covered the Valley. I wish Grandma could see this, he thought. This is the prettiest thing I have ever seen.

While I'm here, I'll look around, David thought as he walked along the hunters' path. Then he stopped again to look at the sea of

clouds around his island. He thought he heard
a sound.

David put his hand behind his ear and listened. He thought he heard a foxhound whine.
He took in his breath more slowly so that he
could hear. It is the sound of a dog, he thought.
It's that way. Then he took a few steps in the
direction of the sound. He waited again and held
his breath so he could listen. It is a dog I hear,

he thought. I know it is a dog. It's out on the ridge. Then David ran a few steps in the direction of the sound.

"Here doggy, here doggy," he called.

But the dog didn't answer him. Then David stood there holding his breath waiting to hear the dog whine. But it didn't, so he walked on until he came to a big log. He sat down on the log to listen for the sound again. And in every direction he looked there were white clouds. The sun had gone down through the clouds, and he felt very lonely upon his island of green with the clouds around him in all directions.

He's not going to whine again, David thought. It's a foxhound down under the mountain. He's been tracking a fox and he's gone. I'll have to go too, he thought. I'll have to go before it gets too dark. I'm not afraid of the dark. But Grandma warned me not to get lost.

Then he heard the dog whine. It was beneath him.

It can't be, David thought, jumping up. Where is it?

"Here doggy, here doggy," he called.

Then he waited but there was no answer.

It couldn't be in this log, he thought. Then he ran to one end of the log to see if it were hollow. He looked to see, and there wasn't any hollow place in the log for a dog to get in. To be sure, he got down on his knees and felt of the log with his hands. Then he jumped up and ran around to the other end of the log.

"Yes, it is hollow here," he shouted.

He reached down and took hold of a piece of log and to his surprise it was rotten. He pulled the piece of log up with his hands. Then he broke off another piece and another. "Dry leaves," he said. He put his hand down on the leaves. "The leaves are warm. Something's been sleeping on 'em," he shouted. "That dog has just left its bed. It's gone back farther into the log."

Then David broke off piece after piece of the rotted log. He followed the big hollow until it ended. And there, crouched back as far as it could get, was a little trembling pup. It whined and shook with fear as David's hands went slowly down to touch it.

"Something told me to climb above this

cloud," David shouted with joy. "I don't know what it was. But I've found me a puppy!"

David lifted the skinny puppy from the log.

"I'm not going to hurt you, puppy," he said softly. "You're starved to death. I'll take you home and feed you. Are you sick? What happened that you've lost your hair?"

The puppy's skin was red and in two places it was bleeding. "Don't be afraid, puppy," David petted. "I've got you. I'll do all I can for you.

Grandma and I will help you to get well."

It was a wild little puppy that tried to get away from David. But it was too weak to do anything. David held it in his arms as he started running back down the path. "I'm taking you home, puppy," he said. "I'll give you sweet milk tonight. Daisy gives milk for Grandma and me and some for Charlie the pig, and she'll give milk for you too."

As he went down into the cloud mist he held the puppy closer for fear it would get away and he wouldn't be able to find it in the mist. "Who left you upon this mountain, puppy? Did the fox hunters do it? Why did they do it—because you don't have hair on your body? You're an orphan like I was. But Grandma took me and bought me clothes. Maybe Grandma can make the hair grow back on you, little orphan puppy. Grandma can do almost anything."

Before David had reached the Valley he was calling the hungry puppy "Orphan."

Grandma to the Rescue

"Grandma, Grandma, wake up and see what I've got!"

David pounded on his grandmother's bedroom door.

"Grandma, Grandma, wake up and see what I've got."

"Just a minute," she said, turning over in bed.

Grandma found the matchbox on the chair she kept beside her bed. She struck a match and lighted the kerosene lamp.

"Now, come in and show me," she said.

David opened her door and rushed into the room with the little puppy in his arms.

"What is it, David?" she asked, straining her

eyes at the squirming object. "What color is it?"

"Get your specs on so you can see," David said.

Grandma reached down to the chair beside her bed and got her glasses. She rubbed her sleepy eyes and then put her glasses on.

"Bring it closer so I can see," she said.

David walked up beside the bed and held the puppy in his hands.

"It's a little hound, David," she said, patting its forehead with her wrinkled hand. "But the poor little thing is nearly eaten up with the mange and he's nearly starved to death. Where on earth did you find him, David?"

"I found him above the clouds in a hollow log," he said proudly. "You know, something told me to go up there tonight. Gee, Grandma, I wish you could have gone with me. The sun was shining on the clouds up there, and it was the prettiest place I have ever seen. I was watching the sunlight on the clouds until I heard a dog whine. Then I went toward the sound. Grandma, I sat on the very log I found Orphan in. I was as still as a mouse and then I heard him whine in the log. I was lucky to find him."

"Have you named him 'Orphan'?"

"Yes, Grandma. Somebody went away and left him on that high ridge," David said. "I think it must have been a fox hunter who left him. He doesn't have a mother and father and I don't either. I was an orphan until you got me. He's an orphan too! That's why I named him like I did."

"I'll bet he's a fine blooded hound puppy, David," Grandma said. "Somebody left him to die of the mange. That's why you found him there, David."

"Can we save him, Grandma?"

"Maybe we can," she said. "He needs warm sweet milk first. Then we'll get Boliver Tussie to help us cure him of the mange. Boliver is the best hound-dog doctor in the Valley."

"Gee, I hope we can save him, Grandma," David said, holding the puppy close.

"You go build a fire in the stove while I get up and dress," she said. "We'll warm the milk for him. Doesn't look like he's eaten for days!"

"All right, Grandma."

David went into the kitchen. He sat Orphan down on the floor while he laid a handful of kindling in the firebox. Then David struck a match to the kindling. As the little flame leaped up, spreading into the dry kindling, David laid sticks of stovewood carefully on the fire. When Grandma dressed and came into the kitchen, the fire was burning and the stove was getting hot.

"Go to the cellar, David, and fetch me a crock of milk," she said.

David ran from the kitchen and soon he returned with the crock. Grandma Beverley took a long-handled spoon and stirred the cream that had risen to the top. She poured a pint of milk into a pan and set it on top of the stove.

"Grandma, do you reckon we can save Orphan?"

"I don't know, David," she told him. "That mange has a good hold on him. When a dog loses his hair, he might be beyond saving. But we'll do our best."

"I hope we can save him, Grandma."

The skinny hound whined weakly in David's arms.

"He got cold up there on that high ridge without any hair on his body," Grandma Beverley said. "That's why he found a hollow log and crawled into it. I'll bet the poor thing almost froze to death up there."

Grandma put her finger into the milk to see if it was warm enough.

"He wouldn't 've lived much longer if I hadn't found him tonight, would he, Grandma?"

"I'm afraid not," she said. "Let's see if he's too far gone to eat."

Grandma set the pan of milk down on the floor, and David got down on his knees beside it. He put Orphan down to the pan.

"Put his nose close to the milk, David," she said. "Let him smell it."

David put Orphan's nose in the milk. And he licked out his little red tongue, tasting it first, and then he began to lap it up greedily.

"Oh, Grandma, he's eating! He's eating!" David shouted.

"He'll feel better after he eats," she said. "Look how raw his skin is!"

"He's bleeding."

Orphan drank all the milk there was in the pan.

"Grandma, he needs more," David said.

"That's enough for him tonight," she said. "We mustn't give him enough to founder him. Fix him a bed. In the morning we'll go see Boliver!"

"Can't we go tonight, Grandma?"

"No, Boliver will be in bed."

"Then we'll get up early in the morning," David said.

"You'll have to go to bed and get some sleep. And little Orphan will have to get some sleep, too, after drinking all that milk," Grandma answered.

"Grandma, can I let him sleep upstairs in my room tonight?" David asked.

"Yes, if you'll make him a bed down on the floor," she said. "Don't put him in the bed with you. We will try to get him well again so hair will grow over his body, and he'll be a pretty hound puppy."

"All right, Grandma, I'll make him a bed on the floor under my bed," David said as he started climbing the steep stairs to his room. "In the morning we'll take him to Boliver Tussie's, won't we?"

"That's right, David," she said, smiling as she watched David climb the stairs with Orphan.

Dr. Boliver Tussie

"Poor little thing," Grandma Beverley said, looking down into her apron. "He's scratched himself with his toenails until he's bleeding again. Poor little thing left on the ridge to die and you found him, David!"

David looked up at his grandmother.

"Grandma, do you reckon Boliver Tussie can save him?" David asked.

"I don't know, David. But if anybody in the Valley can save him, it will be Boliver!"

Grandma Beverley's long dress dragged over the dew-covered grass along the path. She had always lifted her skirt above the dewy weeds when she went to Blakesburg with David. But she couldn't now for she was holding in her apron Orphan's scratchy itching body.

Grandma and David walked around a high rock cliff, and there was Boliver Tussie's log cabin.

"You knock on the door, David," said his grandmother. "Boliver might not be up yet. I don't see any smoke from the chimney. They never get up as early as we do."

David stepped upon a little porch that didn't have a roof over it. He knocked on the door and waited. No one came and he knocked again. David waited and then he knocked a third time. The door opened and there stood the strangest looking man David had ever seen.

"What do you want, Sonny?" asked the tall, red-faced man. He spoke in a soft voice that was just above a whisper. "I-doggies, you got me outten th' bed. Must be something wrong someplace. That's when they come and get me outten the bed and I don't get my mornin' nap!"

Boliver Tussie laughed at his own words. His laugh was a wild screaming laugh like the foxhound's barking David had heard when the hounds chased the fox across his grandmother's farm. Boliver Tussie stood before him, bare-footed, wearing only a pair of overalls with suspenders across his shoulders. There was a long thin red beard on his face that hung from his chin in a long point. The bright red hair on his head came nearly to his shoulders. He had long

arms and thin hands that dangled almost to his knees.

"There is something wrong," David said. "I've found a puppy and it's nearly dead. Grandma says you might be able to save him."

"Oh, I didn't see Cynthia out there," Boliver said, rubbing his eyes and yawning. "Say, we'll do something about that puppy. Specially if he's a hound puppy! Let me see 'im!"

Grandma Beverley stepped upon the porch without saying a word.

"Don't tell me you're interested in saving a hound, Cynthia," Boliver said. "After all the eggs my hounds have got from your hens' nests, I'd think you'd hate a hound."

"But, Boliver, David loves the little thing," Grandma Beverley said, "and I do too! I can't stand to see a hound suffer!"

She opened her apron so Boliver could see the bleeding puppy.

"Poor little thing," Boliver said, lifting the whining puppy from the apron and fondling him with soft caresses. "Where did ye get 'im? He's a hound all right. Who is so evil on this earth to treat a young hound like this?"

"I found him on the high ridge where the fox hunters build their fires," David said. "I found him in a hollow log where he'd crawled to die!"

"I-doggies, I'll put a curse on the heathern who left 'im there," Boliver said. "I can put the curse on any man who mistreats a hound."

When David looked away from the porch, he counted seven fine-looking hounds of various sizes and colors. They were well-fed hounds and happy. They lifted their tails up proudly in one and two curls. When David turned to look at Boliver again, three red-headed boys, all smaller than he was, were standing beside Boliver in the door. They were barefooted and wore overalls like Boliver. Back inside the room David saw two small red-headed girls run across the floor in nightgowns.

"Honey," Boliver said, turning around and looking back in the room, "I'm goin' to dig yarbs and make medicine to cure this puppy. Hear me?"

"Boliver, ye ain't had yer breakfast yet," said a woman whom David couldn't see. "Waste a day on a sick hound and not a furrow plowed for corn!"

"Honey, the ground ain't hurtin' none," Boliver said. "I-doggies, I'm on my way!"

Boliver crawled back under the floor of the little log shack where there wasn't any under-pinning. David looked under the floor and saw the places on the oak leaves where Boliver's hounds had slept. Boliver got his mattock which could be used for digging and for chopping. On one side of the handle there was a blade like that of an ax and on the other side there was a hoe.

David watched Boliver wade through the brier patches barefooted. He walked as well as David and his grandmother who were wearing shoes.

"We've got to find poke," Boliver told them. "We've got to have bear's-paw, snakeroot, and a lot of other roots. And we've got to have some barks too! I-doggies, if we don't do something in a hurry that little hound is a goner!"

"If you can cure my puppy, Mr. Tussie, will you let me bring him to hunt with you?" David asked. "Grandma says you're a great hunter—the best hunter in this valley."

"David wants to catch a coon, Boliver, so he can have a coonskin cap," Grandma Beverley said.

"I-doggies, this October when the pelts get good, David, we'll ketch a coon," Boliver said. "Only don't you call me 'Mr. Tussie.' That sounds fureign to me. Jist call me Boliver."

Boliver shook the dirt from the roots. He said: "Cynthia, you'll haf to let David carry the puppy so you can carry the roots and bark in yer apron."

"Can we put the roots on Orphan now?" David asked.

"Oh, no, David," Boliver laughed. "We've got to dig a lot of different roots and put 'em in a pot and bile 'em. We'll put the juice on Orphan! Say, why do you call him 'Orphan'?"

"Because I was an orphan until Grandma got me," David replied. "Orphan was an orphan until I got him."

"That makes sense," Boliver said. "That's a purty name fer a hound!"

Then Boliver started digging again. He said: "Bear's-paw."

The plant was waist-high to Boliver and had big, dark green leaves.

When Boliver walked under the trees and the tree branches swished around his naked shoulders, they didn't leave a mark. He's a tough man, David thought. I'll bet he's a great hunter. David watched his bare feet smash the greenbrier stools flat on the ground. Briers won't even go in Boliver's feet, he thought. Maybe I'll get to be like Boliver. He does look like the pictures of foxes I've seen, but he's a kind man and I love him. He loves hounds and I do too, and that makes me love Boliver Tussie. They walked on through the woods digging roots and skinning barks from the trees until Boliver said: "We've got the right roots and barks and we've got enough."

"Boliver, we'll go to my house," Grandma Beverley said. "We'll boil the roots on my stove and while the roots boil, I'll get your breakfast!"

"I-doggies, that's better," Boliver said. "I see right now I'm goin' to have a young man to hunt with me. When a boy cries over a hound, he's goin' to make a fine man. Cynthia, I've knowed you fer forty years but I didn't know

you could love a hound. I've allus knowed you were a fine woman but I-doggies you're even better than I thought."

All through the spring David kept remembering Boliver Tussie's words about Grandma Beverley. And every time he looked at Orphan he felt a surge of love for Grandma. She had saved Orphan, and David felt he could never repay her. The first time he got a chance he was going to do something special for her too. She was the most wonderful woman in the world, and somehow he had to tell her so.

Grandma had certainly been right when she got Boliver Tussie to make medicine to cure the mange. Soon the hair grew back and Orphan grew into a pretty tan and white dog.

During the spring months Orphan grew fast because Grandma would give him all the milk he could drink. She fed him home-baked bread, and before the summer was over he was as large as one of Boliver's hounds. Orphan trotted along proudly with his tail in two curls over his back everywhere David went.

When September came and the leaves turned brown, David, Grandma, and Boliver went to the woods to train Orphan. Grandma had told David that Orphan was a smart puppy and that he would make a good hunting hound. Grandma had been right again. Orphan was soon treeing possums faster than Boliver's hounds. Soon after Orphan treed his first possum, Grandma and David began possum hunting together. On nights when Grandma was too tired to go, David went into the woods alone with Orphan. The pretty autumn nights with blue skies, moon, and stars had not been long enough for David to do all the hunting he had wanted to do. Because winter had come and December was here and there weren't many good nights for hunting now.

Leaf-gathering Time

One morning early in December, as David was carrying in the milk for Grandma, he suddenly thought: Before long it'll be Christmas and at Christmas I want to make Grandma Beverley the happiest woman in the world. She has been the best person to me that I've ever known. I want to get her a wonderful present. But how am I going to get a present without any money? We need all the money we've got just to live.

David had been thinking about this present since November. One of the things he had thought about getting for his grandmother was a dress. But David didn't know how to choose one. His grandmother wore long black calico

35

dresses that she made herself. She didn't dress like the younger women who lived in the Valley. She always wore dresses with a high collar and sleeves that came below her elbows. Her skirts were always full because his grandmother was a tall woman and took big steps when she walked.

His thoughts were interrupted as he opened the kitchen door.

"David, this is going to be a fair day and we had better gather leaves," Grandma Beverley said, looking from the kitchen window at the rising sun. "We might not have another day in December as fair as today, and we had better get the leaves while they're dry."

"All right, Grandma," David said. He set the big zinc milk-bucket on the kitchen table. Then he removed his coonskin cap and watched his grandmother dry the last dish and put it in the cupboard.

"Just as soon as I strain the milk, we'll go, David," Grandma Beverley said.

David stood there with his cap in his hand watching his Grandma Beverley strain the milk into a big crock. Then he carried the crock of milk from the kitchen to the cellar back in the hill that was walled with rocks and covered with dirt. When he returned to get the second crock, Grandma Beverley looked at her tall grandson and said: "When you and I work together, David, we can do just about anything."

David smiled at his grandmother and picked up the second crock of milk from the table.

"Of course we can, Grandma," he said. "I've never seen anything yet you and I couldn't do."

"I'm ready, David," Grandma Beverley said when David came from the cellar again. "Let's go to the corncrib and get the rake and a couple of burlap sacks."

Grandma took her long steps, but it wasn't hard now for David to keep up with her. He remembered how he once had to run to keep up with Grandma Beverley. But he could walk as fast as she could now. When they reached the corncrib David unhasped the door and went in and brought out the two sacks and the rake.

"Now where's the best place to find leaves, David?" Grandma Beverley asked.

"Over there on the hill under the white oak

37

trees," David replied. "There's a little ravine down the face of that hill, and the wind blows the leaves in it. Grandma, the leaves are waist-deep. We won't have to do much raking to get the leaves over there."

"David, you've learned fast," Grandma Beverley said, smiling. "Think of your finding a ravine which the wind has filled with leaves. How did you know it was there?"

"When I was possum hunting the other night I stepped down into the dry leaves to my waist," he explained.

They crossed the little stream and started walking up a gentle slope toward the white oaks.

"I don't think we'll need the rake, Grandma," David told her.

"But it won't hurt to bring it along," she said. "We might need it. It might take more leaves than are in the ravine to cover our garden. And, of course, the real dry leaves on top we'll have to put in Daisy's stall. Cows need warm dry beds."

When they reached the ravine, David ran

and jumped into the leaves and sank almost up to his shoulders. He said: "Look how deep they are, Grandma!"

David started filling his sack with the dry leaves.

"Just a minute, David," Grandma Beverley said. "Let me help you. I'll hold the sack open."

"But you can't get down in this ravine, Grandma," David said.

"Oh, yes I can," she told him. "And two can fill a sack with leaves better than one."

When Grandma Beverley waded down into the deep bed of leaves, David smiled. She held the sack against her side with her elbow and stretched it out with her hand. Then with her other hand she pulled the other side of the sack until she made a triangular opening. This made the opening large enough for David to gather a great armload of leaves and put them in.

"Grandma, I never saw anybody hold a sack open like that before," David said.

"Your Grandpa Beverley and I used to gather leaves together," she said. "He showed me how to hold a sack open this way. How did you always hold a sack open, David?"

"Well, Grandma, I put one corner of it between my teeth and then I used both hands," he explained, as he put a second armload of leaves through the big opening. "I watched Boliver Tussie hold a sack open the first night we caught a possum. That's how Boliver held the sack open for me to put the possum in."

Then Grandma Beverley laughed almost as loud as the sound of the wind in the dry brown oak leaves still clinging to the boughs of the tough-butted white oaks.

"You've taught me something, Grandma," he said. "I didn't like to put the sack between my teeth to hold it. I wondered if the sack was dirty. But I put it there just the same. I'll never do that again."

"You've taught me something too, David," she said. "I never thought about letting the wind rake leaves for me. Your Grandpa Beverley did all his work the easy way, but he never thought of your way. We used to go to the woods and rake the leaves with our garden rake. We'd rake

up big heaps and then we'd carry them to the garden and to the stable and bed the stalls. But this is a lot easier and faster to have the leaves already raked."

David was pleased that he had found something his Grandma Beverley didn't know. He pushed the leaves down lightly in the sack so he could put another armload in. "These leaves are dry as gunpowder, Grandma," he said. "They'll make good bedding for Daisy's stall."

"Yes," Grandma Beverley said. "Daisy will love to sleep on these dry leaves. Down under the dry leaves, we'll find wet ones. The wet leaves will be better than the dry ones to spread over the garden. If we get a wind tonight, the wet leaves won't blow away."

David and his Grandma Beverley filled their sacks and then started walking back down the gentle slope toward the little stream. The December sun was high in the blue sky. The wind was soft and warm for December. The long coon's tail on David's cap rode on the wind above the sack across his shoulder.

"This is the right time to gather leaves,

David," Grandma Beverley said. "Tomorrow we might have rain or snow. This is the time of year for foul weather. Just think, it's only eighteen more days until Christmas. I want this to be a good Christmas for you. You've been a fine boy, David. I don't know what I'd have ever done if I had been left alone without you."

"I hope it's going to be a good Christmas for you, Grandma," David said. "You've been good to me, too."

They walked silently up to the stable, and David poured his sack of leaves over the partition into Daisy's stall. Then Grandma Beverley gave David her sack of leaves, and he poured them over, too. All the time they were working David was thinking about what Grandma had just said about Christmas.

I know what I can do to make money to get Grandma a present, David thought, as they walked back to get another load of leaves. He was swinging his empty burlap sack in the wind. Why haven't I thought of it before? The first pretty warm night when there's not a wind blowing to scare the possums, I can take Orphan to the woods and catch a sack of possums. I can cure the pelts in a hurry and sell them to the Darby Produce House. That's the way I'll get a Christmas present for Grandma. I hope a soft warm night comes in a hurry. If it does, I'll get Grandma's present all right.

Fifteen Days until Christmas

This will be the night, David thought as he pushed back from the supper table. This is the night for possums and coons to stir. It's the warm soft night I've been waiting for. Orphan and I will catch the possums tonight.

' Grandma, I must be going," David said as he got up from the supper table. "This will be a good night to hunt."

"But we have plenty of meat in the smoke-house, David," his Grandma Beverley said. "We've got plenty of pork. We don't need any wild meat."

"But, Grandma, it's such a fine night to hunt," David said. "When it's a warm still night

46

and the ground is damp, the possums stir. When the wind is blowing it shakes the dead leaves on the white oaks and rustles the leaves on the ground and that scares the possums. Tonight the possums will go to the pawpaw and the persimmon trees. And Orphan has been wanting to go for several nights."

"Good luck to you, David," she said, smiling as he picked up his lantern. "I hope you catch a possum."

"Won't you go along with me, Grandma?" he asked her, being polite.

"No, I'd better not go tonight," she said. "I'm afraid I can't climb over the hills as fast as I used to. I might not be able to keep up with you and Orphan. You'll get along better without me tonight."

David looked at his Grandmother and smiled. If you only knew why I am going, Grandma, he thought. But you don't.

When Orphan saw David with a lighted lantern, he knew what was up. He came running toward David. He jumped up and rested his front paws on David's sweater and looked up into his face and whined. Orphan was pleased that David was taking him hunting.

"You know when it's a good night to hunt, don't you, Orphan?" David spoke kindly to his hound.

David looked down at Orphan's coat of white and tan short hair. "Orphan, you're the prettiest hound in the Valley now," David said as he patted his head. "And you're the best hound in the Valley."

Orphan barked at David.

"We'll be on our way in just a minute, Orphan," David told him.

Then David walked to the corncrib where he opened the little door and got a coffee sack and a mattock.

"If a possum goes in a hole, Orphan"—David talked to his hound—"I'll dig him out. I don't want you digging and pulling at the rocks and roots with your teeth. You'll break 'em off, Orphan. I want you to keep your teeth as long as you live. You won't be able to fight wild game without teeth. When a dog loses his teeth he is

48

in bad shape, Orphan. Now if a possum goes up a tree, I'll climb it. You know how I can climb, Orphan."

Orphan whined and barked like he had understood what David was telling him.

When they had walked away from the house, David spoke to Orphan again. "Orphan, I want you to find the possums tonight. I want to skin them for their pelts. I want to sell the pelts to the Darby Produce House in Blakesburg and get some money, for I want to buy Grandma Beverley a Christmas present. Do you understand, Orphan? See, we can't talk in front of Grandma!"

Orphan whined and barked again as he looked up into David's face.

"Now, go find a possum," David said. "It's only fifteen days until Christmas and we'll have to hurry."

Orphan ran away stiff-legged into the warm darkness. His nose was in the air and he was sniffing something as he ran.

He's winding something, David thought as he hurried along in the direction Orphan was running. But Orphan was soon out of sight up the Valley.

When David heard Orphan bark, he stopped in his tracks. His heart beat faster while Orphan's barks grew faster and louder.

It's a possum all right, he thought as he waited and listened. He's getting closer.

Then, suddenly, Orphan stopped barking. But he only stopped for a few seconds before he started barking again. He had changed the sound of his barking.

"He's treed it," David shouted as he took off running in the direction of the sound.

David ran under the tall poplars in the Valley where the golden leaves were almost knee-deep. But they were damp and didn't rustle under his feet. He leaped across a little stream and ran alongside a fence. He came to the place where Orphan was barking. Orphan was standing with his front paws upon the side of a little sourwood. David crawled between the wires of the fence where Orphan was looking up into the tree. Then David held his lantern above his head.

"I see him, Orphan," he said. "You can see

him too! There's a big possum up there holding to a little grapevine. I'll shake him down, Orphan! Now don't you bite him unless he tries to run!"

Orphan barked faster than he breathed. When David took hold of the grapevine, Orphan knew what he was going to do. David gave it a little shake but the possum held on. Then he shook the grapevine harder and Orphan stopped barking. David looked up into the tree and his eyes shone brighter than stars as he watched the possum tumbling down like a big gray ball. Just as soon as he fell to the ground, David grabbed his long tail and held him up so Orphan couldn't bite him.

"You're just playing possum," David said as he felt his weight. "It never hurt you to fall from that little tree. Besides, I didn't let Orphan bite you!"

Orphan leaped up trying to bite the possum.

"Behave, Orphan," David told him. "I don't want your teeth to make a hole through his skin. I want this one to make a good pelt. I want it to bring over a dollar. He's a nice possum with a pretty coat of fur!"

"Here's one to buy you a Christmas present, Grandma," David said, smiling as he put the possum into the sack. "Now go on, Orphan, and tree another one. We have to catch three possums tonight. I'll have to skin 'em and cure the pelts before I can sell 'em to Darby's Produce House. We have to hurry. Go tree another possum."

Orphan ran up the Valley while David lifted

52

the coffee sack up and down feeling the weight of the possum which was no longer pretending to be dead but was climbing up the sack. While David was shaking the possum down to the bottom of the sack, Orphan barked again. David could barely hear him. He started running in the direction of the sound.

When David found Orphan, he was at the bottom of a cliff barking under the rock.

"He's a possum all right," David said. "But, Orphan, we can't get him! He's a smart possum and knows where to hide."

Orphan didn't want to leave the cliff.

"Come on, Orphan," David said. "Come on! I'm leaving. Let's go to the persimmon and paw-paw trees! There's not any rock cliffs over there!"

Orphan whined when he came away to follow David.

"You're crying, Orphan," David said. "No use to cry over a possum we can't get!"

Orphan seemed to understand. He stopped crying and ran again into the darkness. He ran away sniffing the warm night wind.

He smells something, David thought as he sat down to rest on a rock. I'll wait and see what he does.

David didn't have long to wait until Orphan barked again, this time over the north wall of the Valley, beyond Wince Leffard Gap.

He's close to that possum too, David thought as he started running toward the sound.

Orphan's barks were sweet music to his ears. When he reached Wince Leffard Gap, he was getting his breath hard and fast. He stopped and listened to the hound's long soft barks above the pounding of his heart. Orphan was barking up a tree in the cliffs above Academy Branch. David started running again toward the sound. He leaped over the small rocks and climbed over the cliffs. He went through wild grapevine thickets. And he came to places in the woods where the last year's winter sleet had broken the tops from the trees. Here were great piles of dead treetops that he had to work his way through. But he finally reached Orphan who was standing with his paws upon the short stub of a poplar tree.

"Oh, look what a possum, Orphan," David

54

cried with joy as he looked up. The possum was sitting on top of the short tree stub, just barely above Orphan's reach. "Take it easy, Orphan! I'll climb up there and get him by the tail!"

David hung his lantern on a little broken limb so he would have light. Then he climbed the tree a few feet, reached up and got hold of the possum's tail. He slid down holding the possum by the tail.

"Look what a possum, Orphan," he said as Orphan leaped up. "No, you can't have him. Another fine pelt for Grandma's present."

David untied the sack and put the possum in. The two possums started fighting. David shook the sack to make them behave. Then he put it across his shoulder, picked up his mattock and lantern, and called Orphan.

"Let's get one more, Orphan," he said, looking for his dog. But Orphan was gone.

He left here in a hurry, David thought. Then he looked at the bark on a tree before him. It was a persimmon tree.

He's after another possum, David thought. They've come here to eat persimmons.

When he heard Orphan bark, he thought he was beyond another hill. He started again in the direction of the sound through tangled treetops, briers, and wild grapevines. He went over a steep bank and down into a deep ravine. Here he found Orphan barking under another cliff. This cliff was not more than a hundred yards from where Orphan had treed the last possum.

"Come on, Orphan," David said. "We can't get that one."

Orphan didn't want to come, but when David started climbing up the steep hill toward Laurel Ridge, Orphan left the cliff.

When David looked up the steep hill, he could see the stars in the sky through the dense woods. The stars looked not more than ten feet above Laurel Ridge. He kept climbing on toward these stars but the higher he got, the farther away were the stars.

"Now, Orphan," he said, when they reached Laurel Ridge, "we're in tall timber. We ought to get another possum here!"

They walked more than a mile around Laurel Ridge. Orphan would hunt first one side of the ridge and then the other. He didn't strike a trail until they reached Sulphur Spring, which was below Laurel Ridge. Then Orphan barked in the deep dark woods. And David waited until he heard him change his bark.

When David got down the steep hill to Orphan, he found him barking up a giant oak.

Can I climb this one? he wondered. He wasn't sure.

But he tied his possums up in a tree so Orphan couldn't bite them through the sack, and he put his belt through the lantern bales and let it rest on his back. Then he started climbing the giant oak. He couldn't reach all around the tree but he held onto its rough bark until he climbed to the first limb. He rested and then he climbed on until he saw a big object near the top that looked like a squirrel's nest made of leaves.

This is a big tree for a possum to climb, he thought.

When David got higher into the top of the big oak, he stopped and took his lantern from his belt. He held it above his head to look at the big object that was moving restlessly up there.

It's not a possum, he thought. It's not gray. It's brown with dark rings around its body and a bushy tail. "It's a coon!" he shouted.

David watched the big coon open his mouth and bare his teeth. Then the coon walked out a long limb in the top of this giant tree.

That limb might split off with me if I'm to follow him, David thought. I'm nearly up to the stars here. But that coon's hide would buy a nice Christmas present for Grandma.

Then David sat looking at the coon out on the limb. This was the first coon Orphan had ever treed. "I hate to leave you, but I'll have to," he said.

Then David put his lantern on his belt again and started back down the tree. When he reached the ground his hands were hot and his legs smarted where he had rubbed them against the rough oak bark.

"He's up there all right, Orphan," David said. "He's as big as you are. We can't get him, Orphan. He's too far out on that limb. I was afraid it would break with me and I'd fall to the ground. Grandma would never know where to

58

find me unless you'd tell her, Orphan. You can't talk to Grandma like I can."

He patted Orphan's head as the dog looked up into the tree and barked.

"We'll have to leave him, Orphan," David said. "We'll have to come back sometime and you can put him up a smaller tree."

Just as they walked down Sulphur Spring Hollow and had reached the Valley, Orphan ran ahead of him fast as he could go. He ran across the pasture field and barked up a little redbud tree. David walked over to where a little possum was hanging just out of Orphan's reach. David reached up and got the possum which was not even as large as a squirrel. "You're the third possum all right," he said. "You're a baby possum."

David opened the sack and put the little possum in with the big ones. He started for home. Orphan trotted ahead of him with his long red tongue hanging from his mouth.

A Hunter Ruled by His Heart

Killing a possum just for its hide, David thought as he walked along behind Orphan . . . killing a baby possum. We don't need wild meat. We've got plenty of meat in the smokehouse. Grandma won't eat possum anyway.

Then he walked on slowly, thinking how the possums lived in hollow logs, cliffs, and dirt holes. He thought about how they had to hunt food at night from persimmons, pawpaws, and old apple orchards. They must often go hungry, he thought as he stopped and took the sack from his shoulder. He untied the sack and looked at the three possums. "If I kill you," he said to the possums, "I'll only get your hides. Kill you for your hides! Every time I wear this coonskin cap

I think of the night Boliver shot the coon from the tree! I think of how much more the skin was worth to the coon than it is to me."

Then David sat there looking at the possums.

"Little one, I'm going to turn you loose," he said, looking at the tiny possum. "I know I'm not going to kill you for your little hide. It wouldn't be worth twenty-five cents. I'm going to let you go back to your mother. And I don't want to kill you either," he said softly to the big possums that were looking up at him with fear in their beady bright eyes. "Grandma wouldn't want me to kill you for your hides. I'll find another way to buy her a present."

Then David closed the sack and put it over his shoulder.

"Shucks, what's the matter with me?" David grumbled to himself. "I've helped Boliver kill possums and never thought nothing about it. Now I catch possums to buy Grandma a present and start thinking about how much they need their hides."

I've got a bee tree to cut yet, he thought. I can sell enough honey to buy Grandma a present. I'm going to turn these possums loose when I find the right place.

When David came to a tree with a bushy top, he stopped. He opened the sack and lifted out a big possum by the tail and set him upon the side of the tree. There he let the possum scamper up to his freedom. He caught the second possum by the tail and put it in the tree. Then he reached down into the sack and caught the little possum around the neck with his hand. He put it up high into the tree where it climbed slowly up and sat down on the first limb, while the two big ones climbed upon the top twigs that swayed to and fro with them in the starlight.

"I feel better," he said to himself. "Come on, Orphan, let's go home."

"David, did you and Orphan get a possum last night?"

"Three possums—and Orphan treed the biggest coon I've ever seen!"

"Where, David?"

"In the biggest oak in Sulphur Spring Hollow," he told her. "It went out on a limb and I couldn't follow. I was afraid the limb would break."

"What if you had fallen from that tree?" she asked. "I worried about you last night. I kept thinking: 'What if something happens to David. What will I do? How can I do without him?' David, I could hardly go to sleep for thinking about you out there hunting possums."

"I know, Grandma . . ." he began but didn't finish.

"Yes, you like to get out and hunt with Orphan," she interrupted. "I know you like to hunt alone. I know you're not afraid in the woods at night. And I want you to stay that way. But I don't want you to get so venturesome that you walk out on a limb on the top of an oak after a coon. What if you had and the limb had split off with you and you had fallen? I couldn't 've found you."

"I thought about that last night, Grandma," David said. "I wanted the coon but I didn't take a chance. I'm careful about risking my life, Grandma."

"What did you do with your possums, David?"

David turned to his grandmother and said: "I turned 'em loose."

"Why, David?"

"Grandma, I'm getting so I hate to kill a possum," he said. "Only way to kill one is to break its neck. Put a stick over its neck and put a foot on each end of the stick and pull on its tail."

"I've always wondered about that too, David," she said. "Your Grandfather Beverley got so he wouldn't kill a possum. He said he always hated to hear one struggle for breath after its neck was broken."

"Orphan treed a baby possum last night," David said. "And I got to thinking about killing it for its hide. I thought it needed its skin more than I needed twenty-five cents. When I looked down at it in the sack, I started thinking about the others too. This is their valley too, I thought. They live here and love this valley and they have a hard time finding something to eat. They must get awful hungry at times, I thought. I started

66

thinking a lot of sad thoughts about the possums. It was the first time in my life I felt that way. So I turned them all loose."

"David, you did right," she said. "I'm proud of you. You're going to make as fine a man as your Grandfather Beverley. And he was the best man I ever knew."

Ten Days until Christmas

"Now go in the corncrib, Orphan," David said. "I'm not going possum hunting tonight. I'm going to chop down a tree. It might fall on you."

Orphan went inside the crib and David closed the door.

Then David hurried to the house.

"Grandma, have you any old rags you're not going to use?"

"Yes, David. What do you want with them?"

"For my bee smoker."

"Are you goin' to cut your bee tree in December?"

"Yes, Grandma."

"But I thought you were going to wait until next spring so you could save the bees?"

"We have twelve beehives around the garden," he said. "And we don't have any honey."

"That's right," she admitted. "We needed money and we had to sell our honey."

Cynthia Beverley turned from the dishes she was putting in the cupboard. She said: "There are some rags upstairs I've saved for rugs. I'll get 'em for you."

While she went upstairs to get the rags, David got down his lantern which was hanging on the kitchen wall behind the cookstove. He took the globe from the lantern and wiped it clean with a damp cloth. The night he had gone possum hunting he had tilted the lantern when he jumped over rocks and had smoked the globe.

I'll have to have a clean lantern globe to see how to rob the bees, he thought. I'll have to have a nice even flame to give light when I cut the tree.

Then he took a pair of scissors and trimmed the charred end of the lantern wick. He put more oil into his lantern from the gallon coal-

69

oil can his grandmother kept near the stove-wood box in the kitchen. He had the lantern ready when his grandmother came down the stairs with a handful of wool rags.

"David, we had to sell all of our honey last summer," she said. "I know how well you and I like honey for breakfast too. The honey money paid our taxes."

"Grandma, I can do without honey," David said. "I didn't mind when you sold it. I know we had to pay our taxes."

"Is Boliver Tussie going to help you cut the tree?"

"No, I'm going to cut it myself."

"It's a big tree, isn't it?"

"Yes, but I can chop it down."

"I'm going with you, David. We'll saw the tree down together."

"Grandma, I can cut the tree and rob the bees. You don't have to go."

"Years ago I used to help your Grandpa Beverley cut bee trees," she said. "We always had a bee tree to cut late in the fall or early in the winter. I'd go with him and we'd saw the

tree down. Then he'd rob the bees and we'd get a few stings. Your grandpa would laugh and I'd laugh. We'd get a big water bucket full of pretty golden honey. I'm going with you tonight, David. I wouldn't miss this for anything. Seems like honey from autumn flowers is always better."

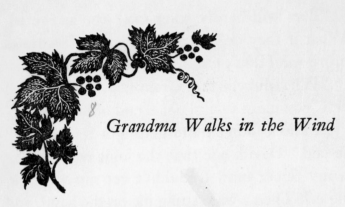

Grandma Walks in the Wind

David left the house with a crosscut saw, ax, and bee smoker. His Grandma Beverley carried the lantern, two large buckets, and a handful of rags. She had a knife in one of the buckets to cut the honey from the hollow tree.

"These are the bees I found watering on a sandbar down in the pasture," David said as they walked along on the clear cool December night. "I coursed them right up the hill yonder to a big holler white oak. That was the easiest bee tree I've ever found. Grandma, there's a lot of bees in the tree too. They work in and out of a knothole high on the tree like a small bright cloud. You might get a lot of stings by coming along, Grandma."

74

"Bees will hardly sting me," she answered. "What if they do? I've been stung a few times before and I don't mind a few more stings."

"What did you say, Grandma?" David asked her. "You mean you're not afraid of bee stings?"

"I said I didn't mind getting a few stings," she said. "David, one time the joint was swollen on my finger until I couldn't get my wedding ring off. Then a wasp stung me on the hand, and my how it hurt! But it made the swelling go down, and I could slip my ring over my finger. Now I've got rheumatics again and my finger joints are swollen. So I want a few bee stings to make the swelling go down."

"Shucks, Grandma," David said. "I didn't know bee stings were good for anything. You know so many things."

"It's the truth, Son," she said. "Bee stings are good for swelling in the joints."

Grandma Beverley took long steps, swinging her lighted lantern. Millions of bright stars twinkled in the clear blue sky to give the dark earth some light. Soon they walked into the leafless timber.

"It's this way, Grandma," David said. "Follow me."

The trees were so tall that, looking up from the ground, David could believe that their topmost twigs were right against the stars. They walked over the carpet of last year's leaves that rustled beneath their feet. There were a few brown leaves clinging to the boughs of the white oaks and a wind rustled these leaves and made a lonesome noise above them.

"We've reached the white-oak grove, Grandma," David said. "The tree is right down here."

David walked down to the big white oak that leaned down the hill. He laid his hand upon its bark. "This is the tree, Grandma," he said. "See my initial on it!"

His grandmother walked up to the tree and looked at the big "D" that David had cut in the white-oak bark with his ax.

"Yes, mark a bee tree and no one else is allowed to cut it," she said. "And this tree is in our woods, David."

9 Blossoms for the Bees

David broke the branch from a little dogwood and hung his lantern handle over the stub where its light would shine on the white oak.

"Now, Grandma, this will be harder than sawing wood," David told her. "Reckon you can hold out to cut this tree?"

"Oh, yes, David," she said, smiling. "I'll take my time. We'll saw it faster than you could chop it down."

David and his grandmother held the saw to the bark of the white oak. They began pulling it across the tree. Slivers of green wood came from the drag teeth as the crosscut ate deeper into the tree. Once Grandma Beverley stopped to rest.

She stood up straight to rest her back because, when she pulled the crosscut, she had to bend over. After she had rested, they began sawing again.

"Grandma, you can saw as good as anybody I've ever sawed with," David said. "I believe you can saw better than Boliver."

"Thank you, David," she said. "I used to help your grandpa. We used to saw down trees and cut them up for wood. It was a lot of fun, too."

Soon the tree started cracking and there was a big split in its trunk. David and his grandmother pulled the saw out and stepped back out of the way.

"It's going, Grandma," David shouted as the big tree started lumbering down through the other trees to the ground.

There was a great swish and the popping of branches, and then the white oak hit the ground with a terrible crash.

"The bees will be all excited," Grandma Beverley said. "They won't know what's happened to their tree. The jolt will wake them from their sleep. I'll fill the bee smoker with rags while they get settled."

In the stillness of the night they could hear the bees making a disturbed noise down in the darkness. Grandma Beverley filled the bee smoker with rags and struck a match to them. Then she worked the bee smoker until the foul-smelling smoke started puffing. "It's ready, David," she said. "We're ready to get some fresh wild honey."

"Grandma, I believe there's plenty of honey in this tree," David said. "It's big enough to hold a lot."

"I remember once when your Grandpa Beverley and I got a whole tub of honey from a tree," she said. "That was a long time ago when there were plenty of wild flowers, when the bees had plenty of blossoms to work on. Our hills hadn't been plowed up then, and people were more careful with fire. No one ever let out a fire to kill the wild flowers and trees that bloomed for bees."

"You use the smoker, Grandma, and I'll chop a hole into the tree to get the honey."

"We won't waste the honey, David, if I help you saw places into the tree and then you split them out with your ax," she said. "That's the way your Grandpa Beverley and I used to do."

"But I'm afraid you'll get tired," David said.

"Oh, no, David," she said. "That was an easy tree to saw down. I'm not tired."

Robbing the Bees

Grandma Beverley took the lantern from the tree and held the bee smoker while David carried the saw and ax. They walked alongside of the body of the tree about fifty feet down the hill. "Here are the bees, David," Grandma Beverley said, as they flew from a big knothole and swarmed around the lantern light. "Look at 'em! They're the big golden honey bees that make a lot of honey!"

Then Grandma Beverley set the lantern on the ground beside her. She put the bee smoker up to the knothole and began pumping smoke back into the log. "This will slow 'em down," she said.

Grandma Beverley smoked them until they

were too sick to come from the knothole. David plugged the opening with sticks and leaves until they couldn't crawl out. Then he hung the lantern in a small sourwood so it could furnish enough light for Grandma and him to saw into the log.

They sawed down into the log in three places. They sawed deep enough to reach the honey, for it was sticking on the teeth of the crosscut.

"Now before you split these pieces from the tree, David," she said, "you unstop the knothole and I'll give them some more smoke! If I don't, when you split out a chunk of tree they'll cover us."

David pulled the sticks and leaves from the knothole and his grandma pumped more ragsmoke back into the hollow tree until the great roar of the disturbed bees became quieter. Then David began splitting the first chunk from the oak.

"David, you can use an ax like a man," his grandmother said proudly as she watched him lift the chunk from the tree.

84

"Honey, Grandma," he shouted excitedly. "Here's plenty of it."

"More smoke, too," she said as the bees started coming out.

Grandma Beverley got up close and smoked the bees.

"Ouch, one stung me on the hand," she said, laughing. "But that is good. I hope one stings my other hand."

"One got up my pants leg and stung me too," David said, slapping his leg where the bee stung him. David turned the chunk over and it was covered with honeycomb three tiers deep. "The buckets, Grandma," he said.

Grandma Beverley stopped using her smoker long enough to give David the buckets. David stripped the honey from the chunk first. Then he started taking honey from the tree while his grandmother began smoking the bees again. When a bee stung David, he laughed and told his grandmother. And when one stung her, she laughed and told David.

He took enough honey from this section to fill a bucket.

"That's the prettiest honey I ever saw," Grandma Beverley said. "David, you'll like this honey for your breakfast. Honey made early in the spring and late in the fall is made from yellow blossoms. It's strange, but wild flowers in early spring and late fall nearly all have yellow blossoms and they make the best golden honey."

Then David split the second section from the log. And he filled the second big bucket.

"There's plenty more honey, Grandma," he said. "We didn't bring enough buckets. What will we do now?"

"But we've got six gallons of honey, David," she said. "This will be enough. We can leave the rest for the bees. You can put the chunks back onto the tree."

"Yes, I can, Grandma," he said. "That will be wonderful too. I'd never have thought of that."

"That's the reason I thought it better to use the saw."

"We won't lose the bees, will we?"

"No, we'll save the bees," she said.

David put back the two pieces he had split from the tree, and they fit together neatly.

"Now tomorrow we can come back and seal the cracks where we've sawed so the rain can't get at them," she said. "I've got plenty of sealing wax. And the bees can live here all winter. And come spring, we can put them in a hive!"

"Gee, Grandma, this is wonderful," he said. "Only reason I hated to cut this tree was losing the bees. You do know how to cut a bee tree, don't you?"

"Oh, yes. I remember from a long time ago when your Grandpa Beverley and I used to cut them, how we used to save bees in the fall by cutting the tree this way. Of course, if the tree split all to pieces when it fell we couldn't have saved the bees."

"But, Grandma," David said, rubbing a spot on his hand where a bee had stung him, "how will we get home with this load?"

"Take the honey and the lantern and come back for the tools tomorrow," she said. "We have to come back and seal the cracks in the tree tomorrow anyway."

Honey That's Not for Money

David picked up the two big buckets of honey and his grandmother got the lantern and the bee smoker. David walked up the hill swaying under the weight of the buckets. His grandmother walked behind with the lantern lighting the way.

"Be careful not to catch your toe on something and stumble, David," she warned. "Don't fall and spill the honey! Be sure-footed, David."

"I'll be sure-footed, Grandma," he grunted. "I've trained myself to be sure-footed when I climb over the rock cliffs at night when I'm possum hunting."

"That honey will come in handy," she said. "That's honey we're not going to sell."

"But, Grandma . . ." David started to say.

"I know, David," she interrupted him, "this is a lot of honey, but we'll need it. You need honey for your breakfast, and I need it in the winter for colds! I'm awful glad you found this tree and kept it until now. It's God's blessing that you did, David. I'll need honey this winter for my coughing. And we'll use it for baking when we don't have sugar."

David walked silently between the buckets until they reached the cleared pasture field. Then he set the buckets down and rested himself.

"How many stings did you get, Grandma?" he asked her.

"Seven. How many did you get, David?"

"Five," he said, as he picked up the buckets again.

"It takes us to rob the bees, doesn't it, David?" she said. "Just think how you have learned to find wild bees. Just think of the things you can do with your hands. And you have so much fun doing them. David, I don't know what I would do without you."

Seven More Days

As David walked over the snow three days later carrying two buckets of milk for Mrs. Orville Byrd, he thought about the present for his grandmother. He milked two cows every night and morning for Mrs. Byrd and he made fifty cents a day for doing this. David gave this money to Grandma. Prices had gone up on everything, and with his hound dog Orphan to feed, it took more money for his grandmother and for him. As he walked, the December snow crunched beneath his feet and the winter wind sang lonesome songs without words in the leafless apple-tree boughs over his head. I can't get a dress for Grandma, he thought. I can't get her a water bucket—we have two. I can't get dishes.

David didn't know where to get pretty dishes like those he had seen in Mrs. Byrd's dining room. He had been in her dining room twice. Once she invited him in out of a storm. Once she called him in and told him what to do with the milk when she and Mr. Byrd were going away for the week end.

When David took the milk to the cellar on this cold winter evening, Mrs. Byrd opened the kitchen door and said: "Come in, David, after you've finished with the milk. I want to see you before you leave."

David put the milk in the separator. And he almost raised a sweat in the warm cellar as he turned the separator by hand. Then he poured the cream in one can, the skimmed milk in another, as he had always done. He washed the separator and then he went in to see what Mrs. Byrd wanted.

"David, I was talking to Mr. Byrd last night and he wants you to cut a cord of stovewood for us," she said. "You've been a good worker for us. Best we've ever had to milk our cows and take care of the milk."

94

"When do you want me to chop the stove-wood, Mrs. Byrd?" he asked, his face beaming.

Here is my chance to make some money, he thought quickly.

"Not until after the Christmas holidays," she said.

"Oh, all right, Mrs. Byrd," he said slowly. David was so disappointed he could hardly speak.

Mrs. Byrd was sitting before her kitchen fireplace. She had a piece of cloth on her lap. It was cloth that looked familiar to David. As she talked to him, she had never stopped raveling threads. She was working on a big cloth, going round and round the square, raveling threads and tying fringes. On a little round table near her there was a small pile of little square pieces of the old wine-bottles design, which was in the big square she was working on.

"Mrs. Byrd, I don't want to ask you a silly question," David said. "But I've seen that cloth someplace!"

"You certainly have," she said, laughing. "You saw it down at the barn. It's a feed sack."

"What are you making?" he asked.

"A tablecloth and napkins," she replied. "Just two feed sacks of the same color and I'll have a tablecloth and nine napkins."

"Oh, they're beautiful," David said so quickly that Mrs. Byrd stopped her work and looked up at him. "I would like to know how to make them."

"Pull up a chair and I'll show you," she said.

She was pleased that David was interested.

"See, David, the sack is sewed up," she said, picking up a sack at her feet. "First you shake the loose feed from it."

"Wouldn't you wash it first?" David asked.

"If you do it won't fringe as easily," she said.

"Turn it wrong side out," she said, turning the sack. "Start unraveling it at this corner."

She unraveled the sack to show him.

"That's simple," David said. "I can do that."

"Sure you can," she smiled.

David watched her closely.

"The sack has two selvage sides, see," she said. "Tear them off so the sack will ravel."

The selvage edges of the sack were woven so as to prevent raveling.

Then she showed David how to ravel the sacks and tie the fringes. She showed him how to take one sack, divide it into three equal parts, then how to take each one of these pieces and divide it into three equal parts.

"Will you sell me two of the empty sacks down at the barn?" David said. There was a new light in David's eyes.

"Go hunt yourself two of the prettiest sacks down there," she answered. "I'll give 'em to you."

"Thank you, Mrs. Byrd," David said, leaving her kitchen in a hurry.

David knew that he and his grandmother didn't have any sacks at their house. David had never seen feed-sack tablecloths and napkins before. But he knew that if Mrs. Byrd made them, they were all right. She had the prettiest house in the Valley. She had the house people came to see.

David went to the big wooden box in the barn where the empty feed sacks had been thrown. And he found two sacks of the prettiest color he'd ever seen. They were the autumn oak-leaf design. He knew these were the right sacks, for his Grandma Beverley had always liked the October days when the leaves turned and the lazy autumn winds swirled them down.

That night after Grandma Beverley had gone to bed, David sat up and worked on his tablecloth and napkins. This was a new kind of work for David. He was very slow at first and he found the tying of the threads very difficult. But he kept on working. And the longer he worked, the easier his work became. He got the tablecloth finished in three nights. On the fourth and fifth nights he sat up after his Grandma Beverley had gone to bed and made six of his napkins. He worked each night until midnight. Grandma Beverley was fast asleep and never knew when David went to bed. On the sixth night, David finished the last three napkins. "Talk about something pretty," he said to himself. Then he took them in the kitchen and spread them over the oilcloth on the table. "Grandma will surely love these."

The next morning when David went to milk for Mrs. Byrd, he took his tablecloth and napkins. After he'd milked and separated the milk, he showed them to Mrs. Byrd.

"David, this is the prettiest tablecloth and napkins I've ever seen," she said. "You have good taste. You selected sacks I have overlooked. How perfectly beautiful!"

When David told her what he was going to do with them, tears came to Mrs. Byrd's eyes. "You won't have to wash and iron them after she goes to bed," Mrs. Byrd told him. "I'll wash and iron them for you. I'll put them in a nice box and wrap them too."

That evening after David milked for Mrs. Byrd, he knocked on the door. Mrs. Byrd gave him the box, wrapped in Christmas trimmings. "Here's a little present for you, David," she said. "I have a little pig out there in a box on the back porch. It is a runt pig. Our sow had fifteen. One more than she could feed."

"Oh, thank you, Mrs. Byrd," David said. "Your fixing Grandma's present was enough for me. But you couldn't have given me a nicer

Christmas present than a pig. Grandma won't have to buy us a pig next year."

David took the present for Grandma and the box with the pig. When he got home he put the pig in the crib. Then he slipped up to his room while his grandmother was in the kitchen. David was as happy as he had ever been in his life.

Christmas Eve was as cold as they'd ever had in the Valley. The snow was a foot deep. And the wind had drifted small white ridges of snow against the fences.

"We are too poor to have much of a Christ-

mas, David," Grandma Beverley said with a smile on her face. "This will be a cold Christmas night too."

"But I have a present from Mrs. Byrd to show you in the morning," David said. "I'll mend the fire so we'll have fire all night. This is the coldest night we have ever had, Grandma."

When his grandmother went to bed, David pretended he was going to bed too. He went upstairs to his room and waited until he was sure she was asleep. Then he slipped into her room and found her shoes under the side of her bed. He put the box on top of her shoes.

Christmas in the Valley

The next morning David was up and had rekindled the fire from the living embers. The bluster of mad winds roared around their house and banged their gates. It moaned through the branches of the leafless sassafras that stood beside the well in their back yard. It was Christmas at their house, all right. One of David's socks was filled with two bananas, an orange, and striped candy. And the other sock was filled with mixed nuts. These were the things David looked forward to getting since he had known there was a Christmas.

After David made a fire in the kitchen stove, he went out to feed the chickens and cow. This was Christmas morning and he was feeding early.

He wanted to give his grandmother time to be up and dressed.

When David came in from feeding, his face was numbed by the raw winter wind. He carried a box into the house. Grandma Beverley was up and dressed and sitting before the fire. She had the tablecloth and napkins on her lap.

"David, look," Grandma Beverley said softly, tears coming from her eyes and rolling down her wrinkled face. "I wonder where this nice tablecloth and napkins came from."

"Made them from feed sacks," David said.

"The prettiest things I ever saw in my life," she said. "Who in the world would have ever thought of making a tablecloth and napkins out of feed sacks!"

Grandma Beverley fondled the tablecloth and napkins like a little girl fondles her dolls on Christmas morning.

"David, what have you got in that box?" his grandmother asked. "It couldn't be a pig I hear grunting?"

"That's what it is, Grandma," he said proudly. "It's a Christmas present from Mr. and Mrs. Byrd. Their sow had fifteen pigs, one more than the sow could feed. So she gave me the runt pig for Christmas!"

"Oh, that's wonderful, David," she said, looking down in the box at the little white pig. "Runt pigs make the finest hogs. We'll feed him after you look at your presents. Go back there and look on the dresser."

"Oh, Grandma," David shouted, setting his box with the pig on the floor.

"Not this watch, Grandma?"

"Yes, it was your Grandfather Beverley's," she said. "I know he'd want you to have his gold watch."

David fondled the watch tenderly. Then he picked up a new pair of pants.

"Long dress pants for Sunday, David," his grandmother said.

David was too stunned to speak. He was so overjoyed that tears came into his eyes.

"I'm so proud to have a son like you," she said. "I'm the proudest I've ever been in my life. You have brought me joy and happiness I have never known before."

Then Grandma Beverley got up and walked over to David.

"Bend down," she said, "so I can hug and kiss you. You're taller than I am now. You're the beatinest boy that ever grew up in the Valley."

There was a new light in Grandma Beverley's eyes, and there must have been in David's, too, as they looked at each other on this white Christmas morning.

Author's Note

I hope you have enjoyed this story about David and his Grandma Beverly because I knew just such a boy very well and I have eaten many good meals cooked by his grandma, using this very luncheon set of the story. I remember the first meal I ate from this luncheon set. I said, "I never saw prettier napkins and tablecloth." And Grandma smiled. "These didn't come from a store," she said. "They are made from feed sacks and they are one of the nicest Christmas presents I ever got." Then she told me the story I have written for you.

Making pretty and useful things out of feed sacks is an old story to most of the 4-H boys and girls and the FFA's (Future Farmers of America), and to all the people in the areas where feed sacks are used. My wife's father, Emmett Norris, was manager of a feed store in Greenup, Kentucky. I used to go there and buy feed for my chickens and for the birds that build around our house. And often I'd see a farmer, after his wife had made her selection, buy as many as ten sacks of the same color and design. I knew his wife was probably going to make window curtains or quilts or clothes for the children.

One of the most attractive sights I ever saw was a little shack down in a gap between two high hills. I walked past it one day in late September when I was going to Little Sandy River to fish. The weather had turned the planks almost as brown as an autumn leaf, and the large oaks around the house had scattered leaves over the yard. And the window curtains were made out of feed sacks in the autumn-leaf design just like David's.

Another time I was visiting friends in a house just outside a city. They took me on a tour all over the house. When they got to their eleven-year-old daughter's room I was amazed at how attractive it was. Then they told me that all by herself she had made the curtains, the quilt, and the dressing-table skirt—all out of feed sacks.

Grandma and David and Mrs. Byrd may not have been the first in this country to use feed-sack tablecloths and napkins. But Mrs. Byrd was the first one I knew to do it. And when she, a smart woman with good taste, saw what could be done with feed sacks, other people followed her example. It isn't any wonder, then, is it, that the feed-sack companies hire artists to design the sacks and that each company tries to get the most attractive designs that will be made into ladies' aprons, babies' rompers, boys' shirts, girls' dresses, pajamas, and lots of other beautiful things.

Jesse Stuart